MAXIMUM SPEED

AWESOME
AIRCRAFT

ROB COLSON

Published in 2023 by Enslow Publishing, LLC
29 East 21st Street, New York, NY 10010

Copyright © 2021 Wayland, an imprint of Hachette Children's Group

Series editor: John Hort
Designer: Ben Ruocco
Produced by Tall Tree Ltd

All rights reserved. No part of this book may be reproduced
in any form without permission in writing from the publisher, except by a reviewer.

Manufactured in the United States of America

CPSIA compliance information: Batch #CSENS23: For further information contact
Enslow Publishing LLC, New York, New York at 1-800-398-2504.

Please visit our website, www.enslowpublishing.com. For a free color catalog of all our high-quality books,
call toll free 1-800-398-2504 or fax 1-877-980-4454.

Cataloging-in-Publication Data

Names: Colson, Rob.
Title: Awesome aircraft / Rob Colson.
Description: New York : Enslow Publishing, 2023. | Series: Maximum speed | Includes glossary and index.
Identifiers: ISBN 9781978530980 (pbk.) | ISBN 9781978531000 (library bound) | ISBN 9781978530997 (6pack) | ISBN 9781978531017 (ebook)
Subjects: LCSH: Flying-machines--Juvenile literature. | Airplanes--Juvenile literature.
: LCC TL547.C66 2023 | DDC 629.133--dc23

Picture credits:

FC-front cover, BC-back cover, t-top, b-bottom, l-left, r-right, c-centre

FC, 12–13, 30 Judson Brohmer/US Air Force; BC, 26 Fingerhut/Shutterstock.com; 1, 16–17 Ryan Fletcher/Shutterstock.com; 4tl Library of Congress; 4–5 Everett Historical/Shutterstock.com; 5tr Slavica S/Shutterstock.com; 6 US Air Force; 7tl Library of Congress; 7tr National Archives and Records Administration; 7b Richard Eldridge/US Air Force; 8–9 Stefan Holm/Shutterstock.com; 8bl Shaneeast/Shutterstock.com; 9t Ryan Fletcher/Shutterstock.com; 9cr US Air Force; 10–11 NASA; 13t Lori Losey/NASA; 13b Brian Shul/US Air Force; 14–15 John Selway/Shutterstock.com; 15b Dance60/Shutterstock.com; 16–17 Ryan Fletcher/Shutterstock.com; 16b, 17t Dmitry Birin/Shutterstock.com; 18–19 Ryan Mulhall/Shutterstock.com; 19 NASA; 20l Everett Historical/Shutterstock.com; 20r Aleksandr Markin/Creative Commons ShareAlike; 20–21 abaghda/Shutterstock.com; 21r Jim Moran/NASA; 22l Institute of Engineering Thermophysics, Chinese Academy of Sciences; 22–23 BAE Systems; 23br Shutterstock.com; 24–25 Baranov E/Shutterstock.com; 27t Marc Lacoste/Creative Commons ShareAlike; 27b KYB/Creative Commons ShareAlike; 28–29 Vittorio C/University of Pisa; 28c Ryan Fletcher/Shutterstock.com; 28b Materialise/Airbus; 29t NASA/The Boeing Company; 29b Imaginactive

Find us on

CONTENTS

- THE EARLY YEARS OF FLIGHT — 4
- ELITE TEST PILOTS — 6
- SECOND WORLD WAR PLANES — 8
- BREAKING THE SOUND BARRIER — 10
- LOCKHEED SR-71 — 12
- SUPERSONIC PASSENGER JETS — 14
- GIANT JETS — 16
- FLYING HIGH — 18
- UNPOWERED FLIGHT — 20
- UNMANNED DRONES — 22
- ROTOR-POWERED HELICOPTERS — 24
- HYBRID HELICOPTERS — 26
- AIRCRAFT OF THE FUTURE — 28
- GLOSSARY — 30
- SPEED FILE — 31
- INDEX — 32

THE EARLY YEARS OF
FLIGHT

The first powered aircraft was built in the USA at the start of the twentieth century. Within a few years, aircraft were being made all over the world, and flying faster and faster. They were soon being used in warfare, and, as safety improved, they developed to carry passengers and freight.

▲ FIRST MANNED FLIGHT

The first human beings to fly took to the air in 1783 in a hot air balloon. It was made by French brothers Joseph-Michel and Jacques-Étienne Montgolfier. The balloon flew to a height of 3,281 feet (1,000 m) above Paris. It was attached to a tether on the ground, and rose up because the hot air inside the balloon weighed less than the air around it.

The all-time speed record for hot air balloons was set in 1991 by the *Pacific Flyer*, which hitched a ride on a group of winds called the **jet stream** (see page 15) to reach

245 miles per hour!

A CENTURY OF SPEED

1913
Deperdussin Monocoque | 127 miles (204 km) per hour

1944
Messerschmitt Me | 702 miles (1,130 km) per hour

1906
Santos-Dumont 14-bis | 25 miles (40 km) per hour

1928
Macchi M.52bis | 319 miles (513 km) per hour

HEAVIER THAN AIR

American brothers Wilbur and Orville Wright built the first heavier-than-air flying machine, the Wright Flyer, in 1903. Orville piloted the first successful flight, remaining in the air for 12 seconds as he covered a distance of 121 feet (37 m) – about the same distance as the wingspan of an Airbus A320 passenger jet.

TRIPLANES

Lift

Just 11 years after the Wright brothers' first flight, planes were used in warfare for the first time during the First World War (1914–1918). Many fighter aircraft, such as the German Fokker DrI, had three wings, one on top of the other. This was to maximize the force of lift to keep the aircraft in the air. It was given forward **thrust** by a propeller at the front, and had a maximum speed of 99 miles (159) km) per hour.

DARING PILOTS

Flying early aircraft was very dangerous, and many of the early pioneers were killed in crashes. British pilot Charles Rolls, co-founder of the Rolls-Royce car company, made more than 200 flights in a Wright Flyer. In 1910, he was the first person to cross the English Channel both ways by plane, completing the flight in 95 minutes. Rolls died later that year when the tail of his Wright Flyer broke off during an air display, causing the plane to crash.

Speed of sound | 767 miles (1,234 km) per hour

1947
Bell X-1 | 891 miles (1,434 km) per hour

1956
Fairey Delta 2 | 1,132 miles (1,822 km) per hour

1976
Lockheed SR-71 Blackbird | 2,193 miles (3,529 km) per hour

ELITE
TEST PILOTS

*Test pilots fly experimental aircraft, pushing the limits of speed and **altitude**. These elite pilots are the best aviators in the world. To be chosen as a test pilot, you need ace flying skills. You also need to be supremely fit, and extremely brave!*

LÉON LEMARTIN

The early pioneers of aviation were daredevils who risked their lives every time they flew. Frenchman Léon Lemartin (1883–1911) tested early designs for passenger aircraft, carrying a record 12 people in his Blériot XIII aircraft in 1911. Like many of the early test pilots, Lemartin was killed in a crash.

NANCY HARKNESS LOVE

American Nancy Harkness Love (1914–1976) was obsessed with flying from an early age, and earned her pilot's license at only 16. In the 1930s, she competed against men in air races, and her strong performances earned her a job as a test pilot. During the Second World War, Love commanded the Women's Auxiliary Ferrying Squadron, who transported new aircraft from factories to air bases. She was the first woman to be cleared to fly all military aircraft, including the latest fighter jets.

CHUCK YEAGER

US Air Force pilot Chuck Yeager (born 1923) made history in 1947 when he made the first **supersonic** manned flight in a Bell X-1 (see pages 10–11). Yeager trained as a fighter pilot during the Second World War (1939–1945). He demonstrated superb flying skills during the war, which led to his selection as a test pilot. Yeager broke many speed and altitude records, and he reached a speed of Mach 2.44 in 1953. Just after reaching this top speed, he lost control of his X-1A and plunged 52,493 feet (16,000 m) in less than a minute before regaining control just in time to prevent a crash.

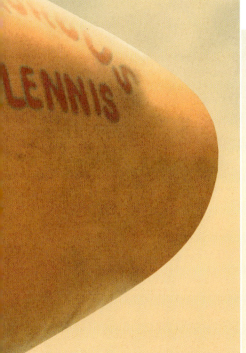

G-FORCES

High-speed aircraft are capable of rapid acceleration. The acceleration puts the pilots' bodies under the strain of huge forces called g-forces. The force equivalent to gravity is 1 g. When fighter jets accelerate, the pilots are placed under forces up to 9 g. Blood drains from their heads to their feet, and they are in danger of passing out. Pilots are trained to withstand g-forces in centrifuge machines (below), which spin them around. Pilots also wear a tight "anti-g suit," which stops blood from draining into the legs.

SECOND WORLD WAR
PLANES

The Second World War was the first war in which major battles were fought in the air. A wide range of aircraft were developed during the war, including fighters, bombers, and transport planes.

▶ SPITFIRE

The Supermarine Spitfire was a British single-seater fighter. It was small, fast, and nimble, and played an important role in the Battle of Britain in 1940, repelling German fighters that were attacking Britain from the air. The Spitfire was one of the fastest propeller-driven fighters, with a top speed of 369 miles (594 km) per hour. It was reliable and cheap to construct, and more than 20,000 were made.

◀ P-51 MUSTANG

The US developed the P-51 Mustang in 1940. To boost its performance, it was fitted with a British Rolls-Royce Merlin 61 engine, the same engine that powered the Spitfire. This gave it excellent performance at high altitude, and the Mustang played a crucial role later in the war on bombing missions over Germany.

A CENTURY OF SPEED

1936
Spitfire | 369 miles (593 km) per hour

1940
P-51 Mustang | 437 miles (703 km) per hour

1941
Me 262 | 541 miles (870 km) per hour

Speed of sound | 767 miles (1,234 km) per hour

◀ MESSERSCHMITT ME 262

Germany made the first fighter jet, the Messerschmitt Me 262, which entered operation in 1944. Powered by a turbojet engine, it had a top speed of 541 miles (871 km) per hour. It was much faster than propeller-driven planes, but it was heavier and less reliable. By the end of the war, all sides had developed fighters powered by jet engines.

TURBOJET ENGINE

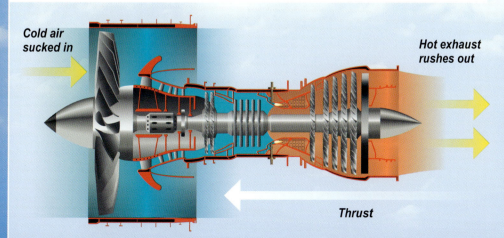

Cold air sucked in

Hot exhaust rushes out

Thrust

Turbojet engines work using Newton's Third Law of Motion, which states that "every action has an equal and opposite reaction." A high-speed stream of gas is pushed out of the back of the turbojet, and this produces thrust in the opposite direction, which pushes the aircraft forward.

BREAKING THE SOUND BARRIER

In 1947, an American Bell X-1, flown by pilot Chuck Yeager, became the first aircraft to fly faster than the speed of sound. Known as "supersonic," this speed was thought to be very dangerous, so it took a brave pilot to attempt it.

THE SOUND BARRIER

If an aircraft is traveling at the speed of sound, it is said to have reached Mach 1. The actual speed of Mach 1 varies depending on the aircraft's altitude. Sound travels more slowly through colder air, and the higher an aircraft is, the colder the air around it. Above 7 miles (12 km), the temperature in the atmosphere levels out at a chilly -60°F (-51°C) until you reach 13 miles (22 km) up, where it starts to warm up again.

Height		Speed of sound
14 km	Yeager's X-1 | 13.7 km	1,062 km/h
12 km		1,062 km/h
10 km	Commercial jet | 10 km	1,078 km/h
8 km	Mt Everest | 8.8 km	1,109 km/h
6 km		1,139.2 km/h
4 km		1,169 km/h
2 km		1,197 km/h
Sea level		1,235 km/h

The Bell X-1 was powered by a rocket engine.

Aircraft are banned from breaking Mach 1 over land except in an emergency – the sonic boom is way

too loud!

SONIC BOOM

The moment an aircraft reaches Mach 1 is greeted by an explosive sound called a sonic boom. As a plane moves through the air, it produces pressure waves that move away at the speed of sound. These are much like the waves a speedboat creates as it moves through the water. If the speedboat is moving more quickly than the waves, the waves forming ahead of the boat bunch up on one another to form a wake, which is one large wave. If you are standing on the shore as a boat passes, at first the water will be undisturbed, then the wake will come and splash you. Similarly, when you see a plane at supersonic speed, you will first hear nothing, then you will hear a loud boom.

1. An aircraft in flight creates a series of pressure waves that radiate in all directions.
2. These waves are compressed the faster the aircraft goes.
3. Eventually the waves merge into a single shock wave.

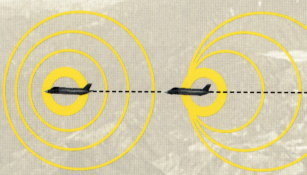

Subsonic　　　　Mach 1　　　　Supersonic

LOCKHEED
SR-71

The US Air Force's Lockheed SR-71 holds the record as the fastest aircraft in which the pilot can breathe air. It was so fast that it could escape missiles by simply accelerating away from them.

SECRET MISSIONS

The SR-71 was a **reconnaissance** aircraft, which flew on secret missions over enemy territory, collecting information. Its dark blue color made it hard to see against the night sky, and led to its nickname "Blackbird."

◁ BURNING FUEL

The secret to the SR-71's speed is its powerful turbojet engines, which are fitted with afterburners. These insert extra fuel into the jet exhaust, creating more thrust. Afterburners use a lot of fuel, and after about 90 minutes at supersonic speed, the SR-71 needed to be refueled by an aerial refueling aircraft, such as a Boeing KC-135 Stratotanker.

◁ RECORD BREAKER

On July 28, 1976, two different SR-71s set world records. One flew at a record speed of

2,193 miles per hour!

The other reached a record altitude of

85,069 feet!

In 1971, an SR-71 flew a distance of

14,913 miles

in 10 hours 30 minutes. That's more than half the circumference of Earth!

▷ LET ME BREATHE

Flying at high altitudes, the pilots had to wear pressurized suits to provide oxygen to breathe. At Mach 3.2, the aircraft's exterior heated to 500°F (260°C). In an emergency ejection, the pilots' suits protected them from the extreme heat.

SUPERSONIC PASSENGER
JETS

Only two supersonic passenger jets have ever been built: the British–French Concorde and the Soviet Union's Tupolev Tu-144. Shaped like narrow tubes, with long, pointed noses and slicked-back wings, these planes were built for extreme speed. They both made their maiden flights in 1968.

TIME TRAVELERS
Concorde was so fast that passengers flying from London to New York arrived at their destination nearly two hours earlier than they had left! This is because New York is in a time zone that is five hours behind London, but the flight took less than four hours. Concorde's fastest time across the Atlantic was a flight from New York to London in 1986. It took 2 hours 52 minutes and 59 seconds. The average flight time for a normal jet is 6 hours 55 minutes.

A CENTURY OF SPEED

Boeing 747
Maximum speed | 614 miles (988 km) per hour

Speed of sound | 767 miles (1,234 km) per hour

Concorde
Maximum speed | 1,354 miles (2,179 km) per hour

Tu-144
Maximum speed | 1,429 miles (2,300 km) per hour

Fuselage

CUTTING THROUGH THE AIR
When planes move through the air, they are resisted by a force called drag. To minimize drag, both Concorde (above) and the Tu-144 had thin fuselages and swept-back wings. Their long noses could be tilted down on take-off and landing so that the pilot could see the runway.

CATCHING THE JET STREAM

When planes fly from west to east, they can hitch a ride on a group of winds called a jet stream. These are powerful winds that blow from west to east at high altitudes, caused by the rotation of Earth. When Concorde made its record flight across the Atlantic, it was helped by a tailwind blowing at 230 miles (370 km) per hour. Flying from east to west, planes fly into the wind and flight times are longer.

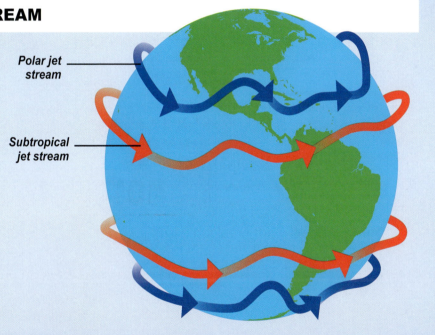

Polar jet stream

Subtropical jet stream

THE END OF SUPERSONIC TRAVEL
The Tu-144 (below) was retired in 1978, while Concorde took to the skies for the final time in 2003. This was the last supersonic passenger jet flight. Both planes used a lot of fuel, and they were cramped inside due to their shape. Also, most countries banned supersonic flight over land because of the sonic boom, so they could only fly at full speed over oceans.

GIANT JETS

These huge planes were built to carry people or *cargo* on long-haul flights over thousands of miles. They are capable of non-stop flights lasting up to 17 hours.

❯ BOEING 747 JUMBO JET

First flown in 1970, the Boeing 747 Jumbo Jet was the largest passenger airliner in the world before the arrival of the Airbus A380 in 2007. It carries up to 660 passengers. When they first started making the Jumbo Jet, Boeing expected it to be replaced by faster supersonic jets. This has not happened, and it is still being built today. In total, 1,555 have been made.

88 m

⌄ ANTONOV AN-225 MRIYA

A one-off giant, this is the heaviest aircraft ever built, weighing 314 tons when empty. Made to carry large cargo, it is powered by six huge turbofan jets. The An-225 Mriya also holds the world record for the heaviest cargo, transporting a payload weighing 272 tons. That's the equivalent of three adult blue whales.

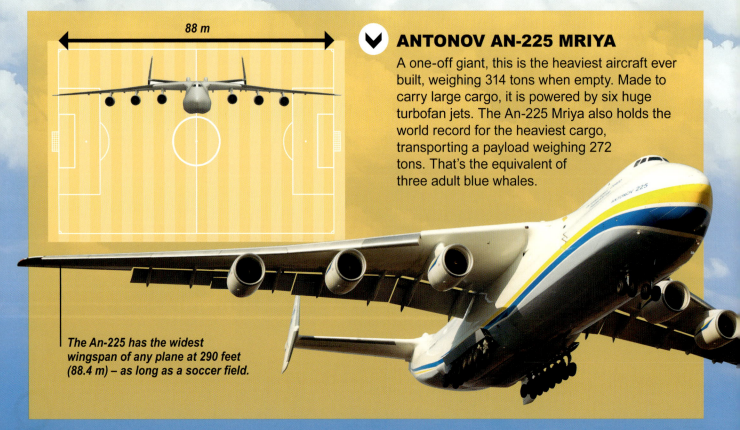

The An-225 has the widest wingspan of any plane at 290 feet (88.4 m) – as long as a soccer field.

AIRBUS A380

The Airbus A380 is the world's largest passenger airliner, with room inside for up to 853 people. Most flights carry fewer people than the maximum as some areas are reserved for first class passengers, who have their own beds.

The Airbus A380 makes the longest commercial flight in the world, flying non-stop from Dubai to Auckland, New Zealand, a distance of 8,823 miles (14,200 km). The flight takes 16 hours 30 minutes.

A CENTURY OF SPEED

Boeing 747
Top speed | 572 miles (920 km) per hour
Range | 8,357 miles (13,450 km)

An-225 Mriya
Top speed | 528 miles (850 km) per hour
Range | 9,569 (15,400 km)

Airbus A380
Top speed | 736 miles (1,185 km) per hour
Range | 9,445 miles (15,200 km)

Speed of sound | 767 miles (1,235 km) per hour

FLYING
HIGH

Some experimental aircraft have reached the edge of space. Many of their pilots are allowed to call themselves astronauts because they flew higher than 62 miles (100 km) above Earth.

SpaceShipOne has reached speeds of
2,175 miles per hour!

RECORD HEIGHTS
Height
400 km

100 km — Karman Line

Lockheed U-2 spy plane | 21.3 km

Highest-ever glider | 15.5 km

Highest-ever helicopter flight | 12.5 km

10 km

Commercial jet | 10 km

Mount Everest | 8.8 km

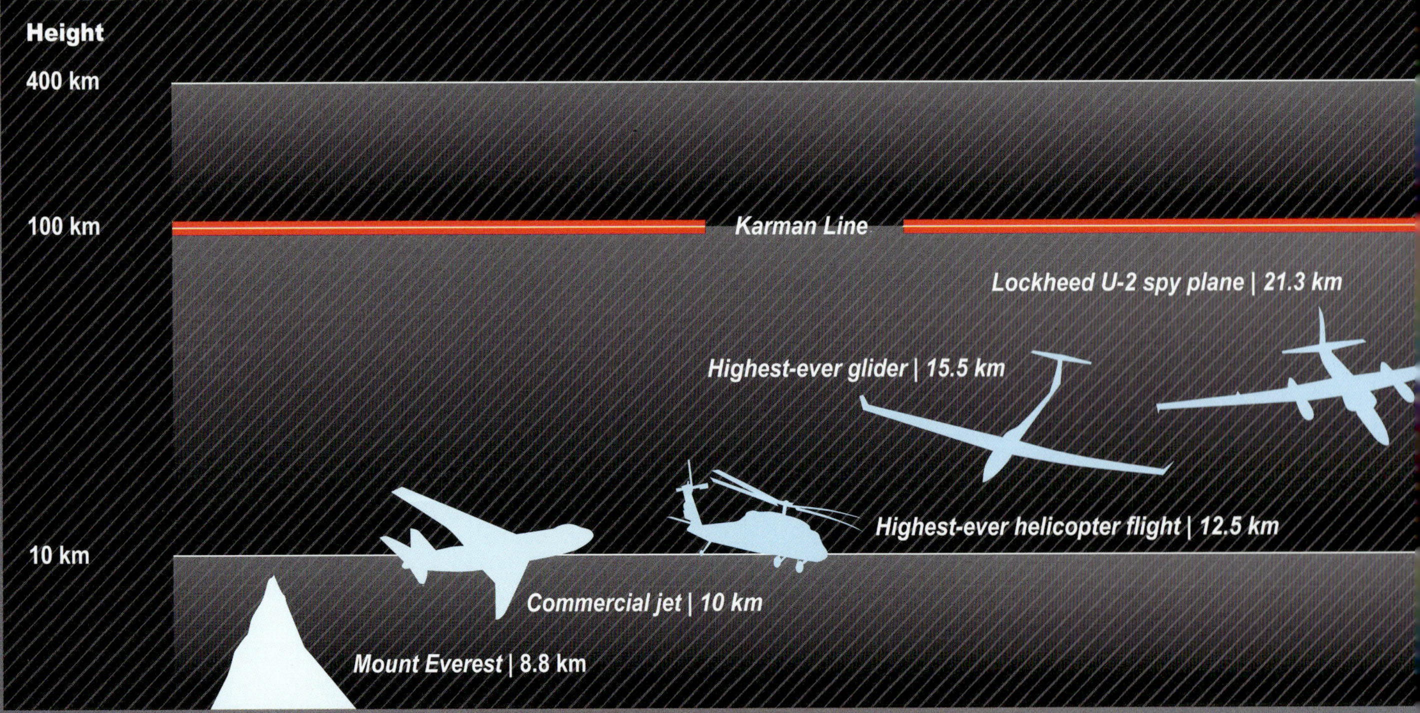

▲ SPACESHIPONE

SpaceShipOne was a rocket-powered aircraft that flew to the edge of space. It was launched in mid-air from a height of 49,213 feet (15,000 m), from the underside of its "mothership" White Knight. It then fired up its rockets to rise up to a height of over 62 miles (100 km), before gliding back down to Earth. On two of its flights in 2004, SpaceShipOne spent a few minutes in orbit before returning to Earth, making it the first privately-owned spaceship.

International Space Station | 408 km

SpaceShipOne | 112 km

X-15 | 107.8 km

The higher you climb through the atmosphere, the thinner the air becomes. The thinner the air, the less lift an aircraft can get from its wings. At about 62 miles (100 km) up, the air is too thin to allow an aircraft to fly. At this point, it needs to reach a speed high enough to enter orbit around Earth. This is the edge of space, known as the **Karman Line**.

▲ X-15

The North American X-15 was an experimental rocket-powered aircraft built by the US Air Force. It flew 199 times between 1959 and 1968. In 1967, pilot William Knight flew an X-15 at a speed of 4,520 miles (7,274 km) per hour, or Mach 6.7, the highest speed for a powered, manned aircraft. Two of the flights passed 62 miles (100 km) in altitude, the height that is officially recognized as the edge of space.

UNPOWERED FLIGHT

Before powered flight, daredevil inventors took to the air strapped into unpowered gliders. Today, modern gliders can soar for thousands of miles at speeds of up to 174 miles (280 km) per hour.

⌃ FLYING MAN
German Otto Lilienthal, known as "the Flying Man," made a series of successful glider flights in the 1890s, reaching heights of 820 feet (250 m). Lilienthal studied the flight of birds, and built his gliders based on the wings of a stork. He held the glider over his shoulders and launched himself into the air from a specially-built 49-foot-tall (15-m) hill.

⌃ LONG GLIDE
German pilot Klaus Ohlmann has broken many gliding records. In 2003, he flew a Nimbus 4 glider a record 1,869 miles (3,008 km), starting from the Andes Mountains in Argentina. In 2014, Ohlmann became the first pilot to glide over Mount Everest.

WING SHAPE

Modern gliders have long, thin wings. This reduces drag, making the wings very efficient. Short, wide wings are better for speed and maneuverability. The gliders very slowly descend to the ground, but they can also rise up if they catch an updraught of air, known as a **thermal**.

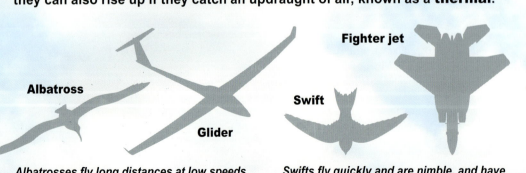

Albatrosses fly long distances at low speeds and have long, thin wings like a glider.

Swifts fly quickly and are nimble, and have short, pointed wings like a fighter jet.

HANG GLIDER

Hang glider pilots fly strapped to a harness suspended underneath a cloth wing. They usually launch themselves from hillsides, but some daredevils start from much higher, jumping from balloons. The record for the highest-ever launch of a hang glider is held by British pilot Judy Leden, who glided to the ground from a starting height of 38,713 feet (11,800 m).

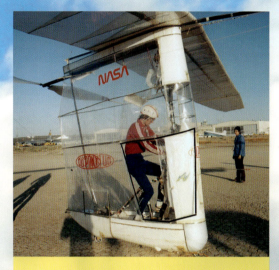

HUMAN-POWERED FLIGHT

In 1979, cyclist Bryan Allen crossed the English Channel from England to France in the Gossamer Albatross. The aircraft was powered by a propeller, which Allen drove by pedaling. He completed the 22-mile (35.7-km) crossing in 2 hours 49 minutes, reaching a top speed of 18 miles (29 km) per hour and flying at an average altitude of just 5 feet (1.5 m).

When starting from high altitude, hang glider pilots wear thermal flying suits to keep warm.

A CENTURY OF SPEED

Paraglider
Speed | up to 37 miles (60 km) per hour
Record distance | 350 miles (564 km)

Hang glider
Speed | up to 56 miles (90 km) per hour
Record distance | 475 miles (764 km)

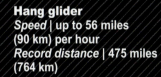

Glider
Speed | up to 174 miles (280 km) per hour
Record distance | 1,869 miles (3,008 km)

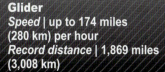

UNMANNED
DRONES

*Unmanned Aerial Vehicles (UAVs), or drones, are aircraft that fly without a pilot. They are either controlled from the ground via radio or operate **autonomously**, finding their own way around.*

AT200

Chinese courier company SF Express plans to make deliveries from 2022 using an unmanned drone. It is currently testing out the AT200 cargo UAV, which can fly at altitudes of up to 16,732 feet (5,100 m). It can fit cargo the size of a small car inside it. The AT200 will deliver packages to remote regions in the Qinling Mountains.

Radar beams bounce off Taranis in all directions, making it hard to detect.

COMBAT DRONE

Unmanned drones are becoming increasingly important in warfare, carrying out secret reconnaissance missions and even dropping bombs. BAE Systems has developed a **prototype** war drone called Taranis, which is shaped like an arrowhead. Its shape has angles that bounce off **radar** beams, making it almost impossible to detect. Taranis is controlled by a human operator from the ground, and can fly close to the speed of sound.

QUADCOPTERS

Drones fitted with four identical **rotors** are known as quadcopters. Two spin clockwise and two spin counterclockwise. The drones change direction by adjusting the speed of each rotor. The record speed is held by the DRL Racer X, which has been clocked at 180 miles (289 km) per hour.

Rotors in red spin clockwise

Rotors in blue spin counterclockwise

ROTOR-POWERED HELICOPTERS

Helicopters are aircraft that are powered by a spinning rotor. They can take off and land vertically, fly at low speeds, hover on the spot, and even fly backward. Helicopters can get to places other aircraft cannot reach, and are often used as emergency response vehicles.

CONTROLLING THE SPIN

In the 1930s, many engineers experimented with helicopters, but they found it hard to make one that did not spin out of control. In 1935, French engineer Louis Breguet's Gyroplane Laboratoire was the first helicopter to take to the air then land safely again. Breguet's helicopter had two rotors, one above the other, spinning in opposite directions, which helped to overcome the problem of **torque** (see opposite).

The Gyroplane Laboratoire reached a top speed of 75 miles (120 km) per hour.

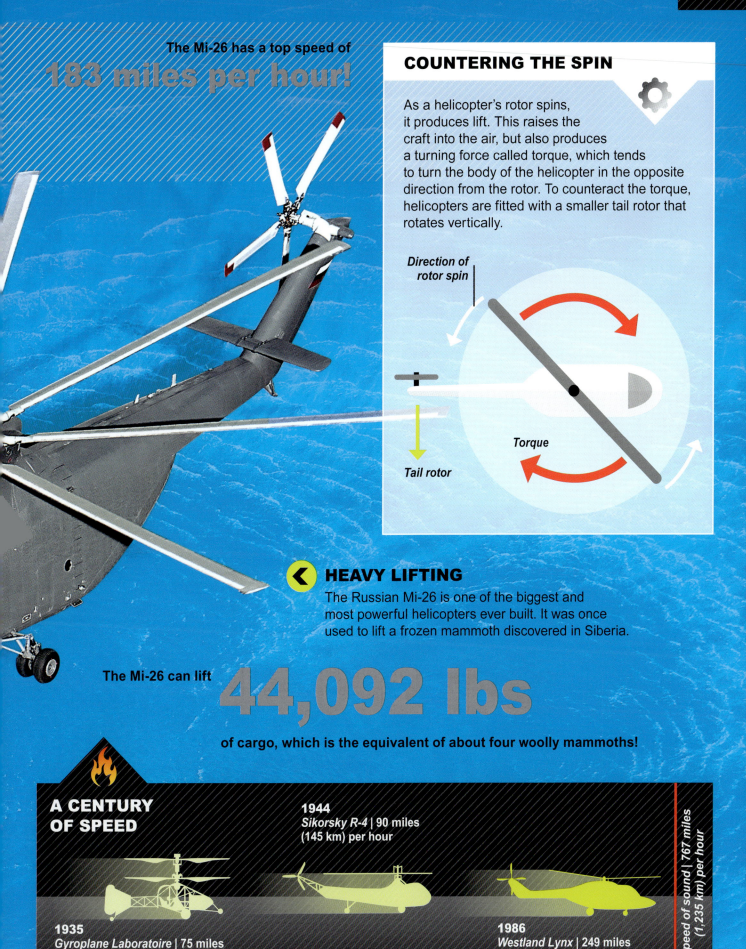

The Mi-26 has a top speed of
183 miles per hour!

COUNTERING THE SPIN

As a helicopter's rotor spins, it produces lift. This raises the craft into the air, but also produces a turning force called torque, which tends to turn the body of the helicopter in the opposite direction from the rotor. To counteract the torque, helicopters are fitted with a smaller tail rotor that rotates vertically.

Direction of rotor spin

Tail rotor

Torque

HEAVY LIFTING

The Russian Mi-26 is one of the biggest and most powerful helicopters ever built. It was once used to lift a frozen mammoth discovered in Siberia.

The Mi-26 can lift
44,092 lbs
of cargo, which is the equivalent of about four woolly mammoths!

A CENTURY OF SPEED

1935
Gyroplane Laboratoire | 75 miles (120 km) per hour

1944
Sikorsky R-4 | 90 miles (145 km) per hour

1986
Westland Lynx | 249 miles (401 km) per hour

Speed of sound | 767 miles (1,235 km) per hour

HYBRID
HELICOPTERS

Helicopters become unstable if the rotors spin too quickly. To increase speed, helicopters need to add wings or propellers. These super-quick aircraft are called hybrid helicopters.

EUROCOPTER X3
The Eurocopter X3 is an experimental design with a main rotor to provide lift and two propellers attached to short wings on either side. The wing propellers counter the main rotor's torque and give the aircraft forward thrust. It has a top speed of 293 miles (472 km) per hour.

The X3 has a top speed of
293 miles per hour!

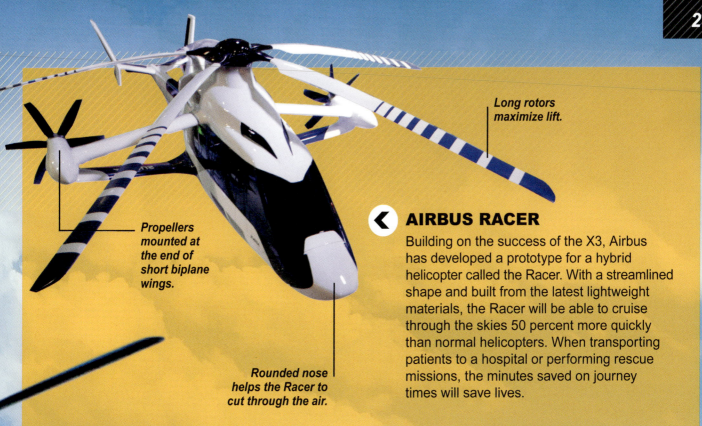

Long rotors maximize lift.

Propellers mounted at the end of short biplane wings.

Rounded nose helps the Racer to cut through the air.

AIRBUS RACER

Building on the success of the X3, Airbus has developed a prototype for a hybrid helicopter called the Racer. With a streamlined shape and built from the latest lightweight materials, the Racer will be able to cruise through the skies 50 percent more quickly than normal helicopters. When transporting patients to a hospital or performing rescue missions, the minutes saved on journey times will save lives.

HELIPLANE

In 1954, Japanese manufacturer Kayaba Industry built one of the first hybrid aircraft, called the Heliplane. It was made by removing the wings from a Cessna 170B light aircraft and adding a rotor to its roof. The Heliplane was intended to have a maximum speed of 106 miles (170 km) per hour, but the project was abandoned after the prototype was damaged during testing. It was considered too dangerous to fly.

AIRCRAFT OF THE FUTURE

One of the main challenges for the aircraft industry revolves around limiting its impact on climate change. Some radical new designs have been proposed to tackle this problem and keep us in the air.

▶ ELECTRIC AIRCRAFT

As they burn their fuel, aircraft give off carbon dioxide, which adds to global warming. In the future, aircraft may be powered by electricity instead. Solar Impulse 2 is an experimental aircraft powered by electricity that it generates itself from **solar panels** on its wings. It has a maximum speed of 87 miles (140 km) per hour. If the technology can be improved, solar-powered aircraft would be a cleaner way to travel.

◀ PRINTING AIRCRAFT

From the earliest days of flight, engineers have studied birds to learn how they fly. One of the secrets to bird flight is their light but strong, hollow bones. Airbus has created a design for an aircraft built of struts that link together just like the parts of a bird bone. The struts would all be made using 3D printing technology.

Inspired by bird bones, this 3D-printed spacer panel is 15 percent lighter than previous designs.

PRANDTL PLANE

In 1924, German engineer Ludwig Prandtl (1875–1953) suggested building a plane with a closed wing. This is a wing that curves right around the plane. Today, engineers are researching the possibility of making giant airliners with closed wings. The design could make the planes up to 50 percent more fuel-efficient.

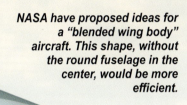

NASA have proposed ideas for a "blended wing body" aircraft. This shape, without the round fuselage in the center, would be more efficient.

> ANTIPODE

Not all the ideas for the future involve efficiency. Some are all about speed. Canadian inventor Charles Bombardier at the company Imaginactive has designed a small jet that he thinks could fly from New York to London in just 11 minutes. Named the Antipode, it would reach a speed of Mach 24 with the help of rocket boosters on its wings powered by liquid oxygen. However, it would only carry 10 passengers at a time. It would also produce a deafening sonic boom!

GLOSSARY

altitude
The height of an object in the atmosphere, as measured from sea level.

autonomously
A way of describing something that operates by self-control, not by an outside force.

cargo
Goods being carried on an aircraft, ship, or other vehicle.

jet stream
Fast, narrow currents of air that blow from west to east high in Earth's atmosphere.

Karman Line
The altitude at which space begins. This is an altitude of about 62 miles (100 km), at which point the air is too thin to support aircraft.

lift
A force that pushes up on an aircraft as it moves horizontally through the air.

propeller
A set of spinning, angled blades that power an aircraft or ship.

prototype
An experimental design for a vehicle that is made to test whether it will work.

radar
A system that detects the presence of aircraft or other objects by sending out pulses of radio waves and measuring how the waves bounce back.

rotor
A set of spinning blades on a helicopter that generate lift.

reconnaissance
A survey of an unknown area, especially by the military, who send out reconnaissance aircraft to discover the position of enemy forces or to map an enemy's territory.

solar panels
Sets of cells that convert the energy of the Sun into electricity.

supersonic
Traveling at a speed that is faster than the speed of sound. When an aircraft flies at supersonic speeds, it produces a deafening sound called a sonic boom.

thermal
A column of warm air that rises through the atmosphere.

thrust
A force that pushes an object forward.

torque
A force that causes an object to spin. The main rotors on a helicopter produce unwanted torque, which is balanced by the rotation of the tail rotor.

SPEED FILE

FASTEST HUMAN-CONTROLLED FLIGHT THROUGH THE ATMOSPHERE
Space Shuttle Columbia
Max speed **17,398 miles (28,000 km) per hour**
Set 1981

FASTEST PASSENGER JET
Tupolev T-144
Max speed **1,429 miles (2,300 km) per hour**
Set 1969

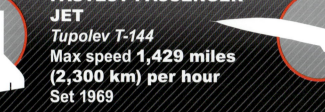

FASTEST UNMANNED AIRCRAFT
Hypersonic Technology Vehicle 2
Max speed **13,201 miles (21,245 km) per hour**
Set 2010

FASTEST HUMAN FREE FALL
Felix Baumgartner
Max speed **844 miles (1,358 km) per hour**
Set 2012

FASTEST AIR-BREATHING AIRCRAFT
Lockheed SR-71 Blackbird
Max speed **2,193 miles (3,530 km) per hour**
Set 1976

FASTEST PROPELLER PLANE
Tupolev Tu-114
Max speed **541 miles (871 km) per hour**
Set 1960

FASTEST FIGHTER JET
MiG-25
Max speed **1,853 miles (2,982 km) per hour**
Set 1967

FASTEST HYBRID HELICOPTER
Europcopter X3
Max speed **293 miles (472 km) per hour**
Set 2013

FASTEST HELICOPTER
Westland Lynx
Max speed **249 miles (401 km) per hour**
Set 1986

INDEX

3D printing 28

Airbus A380 17
Airbus Racer 27
Allen, Bryan 21
Antipode 29
Antonov An-225 Mriya 16
AT200 cargo UAV 22

BAE Systems 23
Battle of Britain 8
Bell X-1 7, 10–11
birds 20, 28
"Blackbird" (SR-71) 12–13
Boeing 747 (Jumbo Jet) 16
Bombardier, Charles 29
Breguet, Louis 24

centrifuge machine 7
Concorde 14–15

Eurocopter X3 26

fighter jets 7, 8–9
First World War 5
Fokker DrI 5

g-forces 7
gliders 20–21
Gossamer Albatros 21
Gyroplane Laboratoire 24

hang glider 21
Harkness Love, Nancy 7
heliplane 27
hot air balloons 4

Imaginactive 29

jet stream 4, 15
Jumbo Jet 16

Karman Line 19
Knight, William 19

Leden, Judy 21
Lemartin, Léon 7
Lilienthal, Otto 20

Messershmitt ME 262 9
Mi-26 helicopter 25
Montgolfier brothers 4

NASA 29
Newton's Third Law of Motion 8
Nimbus 4 glider 20

Ohimann, Klaus 20

P-51 Mustang 8
Pacific Flyer balloon 4
paraglider 21
Prandtl, Ludwig 29
pressure waves 11
propellers 5, 8–9, 21, 26, 27

quadcopters 23

radar 23
reconnaissance aircraft 12–13, 23
Rolls, Charles 5
Rolls-Royce 5, 8
rotors 23, 24–25

Second World War 7, 8–9
solar panels 28
sonic boom 11, 15
SpaceShipOne 18–19
Submarine Spitfire 8
supersonic flight 7, 10–11, 14–15

Taranis 23
torque 25
triplane 5
Tupolev Tu-144 14–15
turbojet engine 9, 13

Unmanned Aerial Vehicles (UAVs) 22–23

wing shape 20
White Knight 19
Women's Auxiliary Ferrying Squadron 7
Wright brothers 5
Wright Flyer 5

X-15 19

Yeager, Chuck 7